A SESAME STREET BOOK published by Western Publishing Company, Inc. in conjunction with Children's Television Workshop. © 1979 Children's Television Workshop. Grover and other Muppet characters © 1971, 1973, 1974, 1979 Muppets, Inc. All rights reserved. Printed in the U.S.A. Sesame Street® and the Sesame Street sign are trademarks and service marks of Children's Television Workshop. No part of this book may be reproduced or copied in any form without written permission from the publisher. GOLDEN®, A LITTLE GOLDEN BOOK®, and GOLDEN PRESS® are trademarks of Western Publishing Company, Inc.

H I J